Nicola Davies
Flying Free

Illus' C th Fih r

Colin knew what it was, even before he took the wrapping paper off off the long, thin box. A gun. Not a toy gun, like the one he'd had when he was six, but a real air rifle, that would shoot tiny lead bullets. Colin was so happy, he couldn't speak,

'Well, "thank you" would be nice!' his big brother Andrew said, grinning.

Colin grinned back, then picked up the gun and pretended to fire it all round the room.

'Bang! Bang Bang!'

'Yeah!' Andrew laughed, 'Bang, bang bang!'

Colin was so excited that he pulled the trigger on the rifle. It wasn't loaded, but it still went off with a loud *crack*. Mum came through the door and almost dropped the tray she was carrying. The cups and plates slid about and Colin's chocolate birthday cake nearly jumped onto the carpet.

'Oh my goodness! What do you think you're doing?'

'Mum, look! Andrew bought me an air rifle – a real one!'

'Yes, I can see that.'

Mum didn't look pleased at all. She put the tray down then stood with her arms crossed and glared at Andrew.

'What were you thinking, Andrew? It's against the law for a lad so young to have an air rifle!'

'Calm down, Ma! Who's going to see him out in the fields? It's not as if he'll be taking pot shots through the cop shop window?'

Colin couldn't help giggling. Andrew always said funny things like that, it was one of the reasons that Colin liked him. But Mum wasn't laughing. Her mouth was set in a straight line, just the same straight line, Colin noticed, as his brother's mouth. Mum caught hold of the rifle and pulled it firmly from Colin's hands.

'Oh muu-uum,' Colin moaned.

'I'm sorry, Col. You can have it back when you're fourteen!'

'That's three years away!' Andrew's voice grew rough and loud; he squared his shoulders and stepped up to his mother. He'd got so tall that Mum only came up to his chin.

'No,' he said. 'No. I saved for that rifle and my little brother is going to have it! Now!'

Mum's face was white and her dark eyes stared, but she didn't shout back at him. She spoke softly, and very slow, as if each word was a little island in the new sea of quiet that had filled the room.

'I'm putting this rifle away somewhere safe,' she said. Then she went out and shut the door behind her.

Andrew called mum a rude word and Colin said,

'Yeah! She is!' but he didn't mean it.

Colin stared at the floor where the roses had worn off the rug and the brown backing showed through. He didn't know what to feel. He didn't like the way Mum and Andrew argued these days, with Andrew looking so big and Mum so small. But he did want that air rifle.

When Mum got back she poured tea and lit the candles on the cake; she and Andrew sang 'Happy Birthday' together when Colin blew them out. Then they turned on the telly and Andrew fed the fire and made it roar in the grate like a lion. But somehow, the room still felt cold.

When it was time for bed, Colin leaned down to kiss Mum's cheek

'Thanks for the cake,' he said.

'That's all right, my duck.' She smiled. 'Sleep tight, birthday boy.'

Andrew followed Colin to the bottom of the stairs and whispered in his ear.

'Don't you worry,' he breathed, 'I'll find it! Then I'll show you how to use it!'

Mrs Calvin was reading aloud to the class. It was something to do with wizards or elves. Colin hated every word. Why couldn't she read about something real?

Colin looked out of the window. The sky was grey and the village beyond the school field was fuzzy with mist. The light was already fading. Would it be too dark for Andrew to give him his first shooting lesson? Would Andrew even be able to find the rifle? Colin's stomach knotted with excitement and anxiety.

'Colin! Colin! Colin!'

Mrs Calvin was standing beside his desk.

'I don't think you've been listening, have you?' she said. Behind her back, Martin Sorsby was holding up a piece of paper that said 'Colin Hocking Village Idiot'. All the children were smirking and making faces at him, but Colin didn't care because the bell had rung and he was free again.

Colin was supposed to wheel his bike down the rough track that led to their bungalow.

'I can't afford new wheels if you wreck 'em going over ruts,' Mum always said.

But Mum wasn't due home for hours and hours, and Andrew's rusty pickup was already parked by the bungalow door! Colin rattled over the bumps and potholes, pedalling hard.

Whhhtt, plink.

A sound like a fast whiplash, followed by a tinny clank, came from the back garden. Colin ran round and found Andrew aiming the rifle at a line of beer cans set up on the wall.

'It was under her bed!' said Andrew, 'Easy!' He aimed again.

Whhhtt, said the rifle, but there was no answering *plink.* Andrew had missed.

'Must be slipping!' said Andrew. He dragged on his cigarette then offered it to Colin, 'Wanna smoke?'

Colin shook his head. Mum had what she called an 'infallible technique' for telling if he'd been smoking: she sniffed his fringe. And anyway, Colin didn't like the smell of Andrew's weird roll-ups.

'Okey dokey, pardner!' said Andrew. Colin grinned; Andrew's American accent was rubbish, but funny.

'Set up them beer cans and we'll have us some shootin'!' Andrew yelped like a cowboy rounding up mavericks, and Colin yelped too.

'Yee haaa!' said Andrew.

The bullets for the air rifle weren't bullet shaped. They weren't even called bullets. They were round-ended, with a little waist like a fat lady in a skirt, and called pellets. You 'broke' the rifle over your knee to open it, so that you could put a pellet into the bottom of the barrel, where it fitted snugly. Then you cracked the rifle back together and took aim by looking down the line of the barrel, to the 'sight' that stood up like a tiny tusk at the end. When the sight lined up with the beer can, you squeezed the trigger, slow and steady, trying not to let any part of your body wobble. And when you'd squeezed the trigger tight, it fired – the compressed air inside the rifle pushed the pellet out, *whhhhttt*. If your aim was good, there was a metallic *plink* and the beer can jumped off the wall as it was hit.

At first Colin got *whhtts* but no *plinks*; the rifle wobbled when he held it, he couldn't seem to line up the sight with anything, and when he reloaded, he got the pellet the wrong way round. But Andrew didn't get cross. He just rolled another ciggy and explained, all over again, what Colin had to do.

'You got to get the butt tucked right into your shoulder. That's better. Then you get your eye right down, onto the barrel, then hold steady...and squeeze!'

Whhhttt, plinkkk.

The beer can somersaulted off the wall, and Andrew whooped.

'Good shootin', pardner. Let's see if you can do it again!'

Colin reloaded.

Whhttt, plink. And again, *whhtt, plink, whhtt, plink.*

Colin sent eight beer cans over the wall, one after another. Andrew set them up again, and, almost as fast, Colin shot them down. Andrew laughed and shook his head.

'That's scary, that is,' Andrew said in his real voice, 'took me months to get half as good! Wow, little bro, you're a natural shot!'

Colin just grinned. He could hardly believe it. He'd never found anything at all that he could just do, without really trying.

It got too dark for shooting and they went inside. They cleaned the rifle and slid it back carefully under Mum's bed.

'But now we know where to find it!' Andrew winked.

Andrew took two cans of beer from the fridge and opened them both.

'We got to celebrate you being a dead shot!' he said.

They slumped on the sofa together, watching telly and drinking from their cans. Colin was dizzy with happiness. He was a 'natural' at shooting; better than most grown-ups. And he was drinking with his big brother, as if they had both come in from work in the fields.

They were still celebrating when Mum came home from work. She walked into the sitting room and flicked on the lights.

'What's been going on here?'

She looked at the empty cans and the crisp packets.

'Nobody thought to put the dinner in the oven?'

Guiltily, Colin remembered the note on the kitchen table: Put shepherd's pie in oven, gas mark 5.

He was about to say sorry, but Andrew spoke up.

'Forget it, Ma. Who cares? We can get chips from the pub if we get hungry.'

Mum snapped off the telly and stood in front of the sofa, staring hard at Andrew.

'I hope you haven't been giving Colin beer?!' she said.

'Oh, calm down,' said Andrew, but Mum wasn't ready to be calm.

'What were you thinking, giving a little child alcohol?'

She spoke as if Colin wasn't there, or as if he was just a baby, fed from a spoon. Suddenly, Colin felt very angry with Mum. He looked at her, standing there with her coat still on and her hair tangled by the wind and rain. She looked, Colin thought, like a witch from Mrs Calvin's daft stories.

'I drank the beer,' Colin told her, 'Andrew didn't make me do anything!' Then he stumped upstairs without saying goodnight to anyone.

Colin's stomach sloshed with beer bubbles and crisps and kept him awake. He heard Andrew leave for milking at five, then he slept at last and only woke when Mum was knocking on his door.

'I've got to get off for work now, Col. Hurry up or you'll be late for school!'

The back door closed and Mum's bike wheels crunched on the path. That meant he had less than half an hour to dress, eat breakfast and cycle to school. He lay still and listened to the silence in the house. He thought about the names they called him at school, 'farm boy', village idiot', 'hay seed'. He thought about Mum calling him 'a little child'. Well, he'd show them. He wasn't any of those things. He was Colin, the natural dead shot. What about that?

He dressed quickly in his oldest jeans and warmest sweater, then ate some cold shepherd's pie straight from the dish and left his dirty spoon stuck in the middle, like a flagpole. Mum would be furious when she saw it. Good. He put on his boots and then remembered that he hadn't fetched the rifle. So, he tramped into Mum's room without bothering to take his boots off and left muddy prints on her carpet. The rifle was just where he and Andrew had left it, pushed up next to the old tent and the folded cot that had been both the brothers' when they were babies. The box of pellets was hidden in Andrew's spare overalls on the peg by the back door. Colin took a fistfull and shoved them into his pockets.

He pulled on his jacket and left the house. The door

slammed behind him and he remembered his key was in the pocket of his school trousers. He shrugged. What did it matter? He could shoot his lunch if he got hungry and cook it on a fire in the fields. He could be an adventurer, an explorer, a pioneer, he didn't need anything except his rifle.

Colin climbed the stile at the end of the garden and left his usual weekday morning far behind. The familiar tangle of hedgerow and copse and the curved lines of the hilly fields opened to him, suddenly as inviting as a whole new continent.

Colin had never taken much notice of the countryside before. It was just the place where he lived. When he wasn't in school he liked to cycle round the lanes, imagining that he was driving the big motorbikes and flashy sports cars that his brother dreamed of owning. Sometimes, he got a ride in the new tractor that Andrew drove up at the farm. It had a radio and a heater, so you could shut the cab door and be in a little world of your own, high above the mud and the puddles. Mum went for walks over the fields and farm tracks on her days off. She picked elderflowers for cordial in the spring and blackberries for pies in the autumn, but sometimes she just 'went for walk'. Colin had never seen the point of that.

But now he was being a hunter, and hunters had to walk

and they had to look hard at things. Finding 'game' was difficult. Animals and birds didn't want to be seen. Colin knew he had to be stealthy and he had to use his eyes and ears as never before. So he took care to notice the racing clouds that sent shadows up and down the hillsides and the purplish look to the bare twigs and branches.

He tried to remember all the things that wildlife and bushcraft programmes on TV told you to do. Camouflage. That was important. It meant blending in with the background so animals didn't see you. His black jacket wasn't too bad for that, but the pale blue jeans were hopeless. He stopped and rubbed the clean blue with mud. His face must look really white, so he muddied that as well. It felt wonderful to be getting very dirty on purpose.

Being quiet was important too, so he walked slowly up the hill, being careful not to tread on twigs.

He reached the little copse of trees at the top of the field and slipped in between the trunks. There'd be 'game' in here for sure! Better load the rifle to be ready. He broke the gun across his knee. *Crack!* The sound it made seemed so loud out here! Every animal for miles around must have heard it. He rummaged in his pocket for a pellet and the rustling of his clothes was deafening.

With the rifle loaded, he stood quite still and listened. The wind moved the twigs in the tops of the trees with a sad sighing sound. Something moved in the thicket ahead of him, a shape, an animal! He raised the rifle and squeezed the trigger. The pellet *phhutted* through the tangle of branches and a large dead leaf fell to the ground a few meters away. He reloaded, then waited for the quiet to close around him again. But the moment he began to move he was making a whole load of noise. It was impossible to walk on dead leaves silently. He scrunched his way to the other side of the copse, angry with himself for the clumsy racket he was making.

Walking along beside the trees was much easier. The wet grass made quiet movement possible, but he could still look into the copse and spot anything moving there. He stalked up and down the woodland rim for ages, sure that some big animal would step out of a bush and let him shoot it. But there was nothing.

It began to rain. The leafless trees made a poor shelter, so Colin ran across the next field to an old barn. It was nice to stand in the dry, hear the water pattering on the tin roof and look out at the wet world. Colin watched the shower move over one hillside and on to the next. It was like a set of misty grey curtains, slanting where the wind blew them and falling one behind the other as the rain spread. Colin could even see the rain coming out of the ragged edge of the clouds. He was fascinated.

Then, almost as soon as it began, it stopped. The wispy clouds looked empty and the curtains dissolved, one after another, until just one remained. The wind pushed that away and white sunlight splashed down from the sky instead. Looking out, Colin was dazzled.

Then, right in the middle of the dazzle, quite close, there were swirls of movement. As Colin's eyes got used to the brightness he saw wings flapping and folding. A flock of birds was landing right in front of his hideout. He wondered what they were. Bird names he'd heard all his life swam in his head – robin, blackbird, thrush, magpie. He didn't think any of the names he knew fitted these fat, contented looking birds with their smart white collars and neat grey backs.

He hadn't really imagined shooting something as small as a bird. But these birds were quite big. What was more, it was clear they couldn't see him here in the the shadows of the old barn. They'd never even know what had hit them!

Slowly, very slowly, he crouched and rested the rifle on some old bales to steady it. Then he looked down the long barrel to line up the little tooth of the sight with one of the birds and took aim. But before he could fire, the birds took flight. Their wings burst from their sides with a sound like sudden clapping. The smooth, round shapes, so easy to aim at, had gone and everything was moving. Colin didn't have time to work out why, all he knew was that his chance was flying away. He fixed on a dark shape that was moving through the flock like a fat arrow. He lined up the sight and shot. *Thhwakkk.* The dark shape fell through the escaping birds.

The bottom of Colin's stomach felt as if it had fallen away. He'd hit something. Really hit something.

Colin leapt the bales and ran towards the spot. There, in the rough grass, was the bird he had shot. It wasn't dead. It lay on its back with its wings spread out around it, not a fat, comfortable creature at all. This bird looked viscious! Colin stepped back in fear, then stood rooted to the spot, staring.

The bird had skinny yellow legs and feet, with claws like curved needles. Its cream breast was striped with chestnut and its wings were barred with brown. But its face was the most amazing thing about it. It had a short, hooked beak, like a disapproving nose, and a pair of bright orange eyes. Its wings flailed, its claws grabbed, it opened its beak and shrieked and its eyes blazed with fury.

Colin had no idea what to do. This was nothing like the vague imaginings he'd had about shooting something and cooking it. There was far too much spite in this creature for it to be edible! And anyway, it wasn't dead. He could at least do something about that. He reloaded, then came as close as he dared to the screaming bird and carefully took aim. First he aimed at the stripey breast and then at the head, between those two orange eyes. The eyes filled his sight, it was like looking into the heart of a fire.

The bird stopped screaming. Its perfect coat of feathers was a little crumpled and it was panting. Then it shut its eyes, just for a moment, and gave a little shudder. Colin noticed that, actually, it was quite small, fragile-looking in fact.

He dropped the gun. His hands were shaking so much now that it was useless trying to hold it. There was a spot of blood on the bird's right wing, and it was growing larger. How could he have done that? Suddenly, Colin couldn't bear the thought that this wild, lovely creature was going to die because of him.

People who had been in accidents had to be kept warm. He'd heard Mum say that. And broken legs and arms needed to be kept still. Maybe that worked for birds too. He took off his coat and then his jersey. Very gently, he covered the bird with the sweater. The claws grabbed onto it as if trying to wring the life out of an enemy. He'd picked up chickens many times when Mum used to keep them and hoped that 'wings folded' was the right way to carry other birds too. He wrapped the sweater arms around the bird, making it into a kind of loose parcel. Then he put on his coat, tucked the bird inside it and began to run.

He cycled so hard he thought his heart might burst, down the lanes and into the village. There was no point trying to hide from school; the vet's house was opposite the playground and as it was afternoon break, everyone saw him rush into the surgery.

There was no one in the waiting room and the receptionist had gone home. The vet was Martin Scorsby's father, but that couldn't be helped. He was washing his hands in a big sink in one of the treatment rooms.

'Please,' said Colin. 'Please help. It's been shot.'

Mr Scorsby wasn't much like his son. He didn't say anything unkind, even when Colin told him his name. He didn't even call him stupid when he didn't know what the bird was called. He just took the jersey-bird parcel and began to open it. The bird inside began to shriek again.

'Oh,' said Mr Scorsby, 'bird of prey, sparrowhawk by the sounds of things. Right.'

He put on a pair of thick leather gloves and grinned at Colin.

'They can do serious damage when they're cross. And this one sounds very cross indeed.'

The hawk tried to flap as soon as it was free of the sweater, but Mr Sorsby folded its wings against its body and held it firmly in one large hand.

'Steady, girl!' he said.

'How d'you know it's a girl?'

'Her colour – males are slatey on the back. And her size. The boys are a lot smaller than girls. Not like humans!'

The vet gave Colin another pair of leather gloves to put on and showed him how to hold the hawk, just as he was doing. Colin had to use both hands and the hawk struggled, but he held her firm.

'Just remember not to squeeze, you need to hold her, not squash her.'

Mr Scorsby reached for a cannister of gas with a long tube and a tiny face mask attached.

'We just need to put her out, so she doesn't struggle and hurt herself.'

In a second, the hawk was limp in Colin's hands.

'Right, lets have a look.'

The vet laid the bird on the treatment table and stretched out her wings.

'Hmmmm,' he said, 'some moron's been out with an airgun.' Colin felt himself blushing scarlet.

'Where d'you find her?' the vet asked.

'Out the back of my house, Ridge Bungalow.'

'Oh, yes. I know your brother Andrew, cowman at Ridge Farm.'

Now Mr Scorsby looked up. 'This isn't his handywork, is it?'

Colin shook his head, but the vet looked at him carefully. 'Did you shoot her?' he said.

Colin nodded miserably. He looked at the green lino.

Mr Scorsby sighed.

'Well,' he said, 'at least you've been honest. I expect you know it's illegal for a boy your age to have an air rifle?'

Colin nodded.

'And I don't suppose for a second you can afford to pay me.'

Colin didn't look up, but he answered in the bravest voice he could manage.

'No,' he said, 'but I can work. Odd jobs, gardening. I'll do whatever you want. Just please make the hawk better.'

'Alright. Look, here's what we'll do. You did the damage. Now you have to put it right. You are going to mend her broken wing.'

Colin looked at the vet in astonishment.

'C'mon,' said Mr Scorsby, 'you made a good job of wrapping her up to bring her here. I think you might have a natural talent for this. I'll show you what to do.'

The air gun pellet had broken the bone in the first part of the left wing and left a nasty wound. Colin had to clean away the blood with cotton wool and antiseptic, then trim

the feathers so the vet and he could see into the hole that the pellet had made. Colin took the tweezers that Mr Sorsby gave him and picked out the pellet; it wasn't very far in and it came out cleanly. Then Colin helped the vet put in a splint to hold the two ends of broken wing bone together.

'Can you sew?' Mr Scorsby asked.

'A bit. I can do buttons.'

'Right, then you can sew up this wound.'

It felt weird sewing up an animal, but the surgical thread pulled the broken skin together, closing up the pellet hole like a patch on trousers.

'Good work, Colin,' said Mr Scorsby, 'now we need to make sure she doesn't try flapping until that break is mended!'

Colin held the unconcious bird whilst the vet bandaged her closed wings against her sides.

'Now we'll pop her in a nice dark cage, so she'll rest when she comes round. You call by tomorrow after school and see how she's doing.'

Colin nodded, then stood staring down at the floor again. He didn't know what to say; 'thanks' just didn't seem enough.

'Don't worry about her,' said Mr Scorsby, 'it could have been a lot worse. Good thing you're a better vet than you are a hunter!'

The next day, Colin was in trouble with everyone. With Mum and with school for bunking off, and with Andrew for leaving the air rifle in the middle of a field (though Mum said it served him right for getting such a stupid present). Colin said sorry to everyone. And he was truly sorry, but the person he most wanted to say sorry to couldn't understand him: the sparrowhawk.

Colin visited her every day after school. Her cage was at the end of the Scorsby's garden, behind the surgery. The wall of the cage facing the house was boarded up, so that she couldn't see people and get scared. Colin had to peep at her through a hole and put her food in through a small hatch.

At first, she had just sat on her perch, hunched up and still. When he gave her food – a bit of dead rabbit – she hardly took any notice. Worst of all, her eyes were dull, like the fire in them had gone out.

But day by day she got her appetite back, until she chittered with excitement when the food door opened and Colin pushed the rabbit inside. She sat alert on her perch with her longs legs straight and their feathery covers neatly preened, like stripey leggings. Her lovely orange eyes had lit up again with that fire-like glow.

After a week, she'd pulled her bandages to pieces and freed her wings. The feathers over the wound were growing back and, although they had turned white, they were smooth and healthy. Martin watched her through the peephole, hoping that she'd stretch and flap them to get them ready to use again. But she didn't. When he put in her food, she hopped down to it like always, as if she had forgotten she even had wings.

'Why doesn't she fly?' he asked the vet.

'They often don't after an injury. She'll have to go to the zoo if she can't fly.'

Colin was horrified.

'A zoo!'

'Well, she can't live at the back of the surgery forever, Colin,' said Mr Sorsby, 'no matter how much work you do for me!'

Colin cycled home, miserable. She had to fly. There had to be a way. By the time he got home, he had a plan. He explained it to Mum and Andrew at tea time.

'If she can see where she used to live,' he said, 'she might remember about flying.'

'Well, I suppose it might work,' said Mum.

'Where're you going to keep her? In the chicken shed?' Andrew smirked through a mouthful of chips.

'I thought we could build her a cage, a big one. There's a roll of chicken wire and some wood in the shed.'

'We? Who's we?' said Andrew. He looked funny with his eyebrows raised, they disappeared under his fringe. Colin grinned.

'You and me,' Colin said. 'Pardner!'

Andrew tried to look cross, but it didn't work.

'After all the hassle you caused running off with that air gun...'

'After all the trouble you caused by buying it, Andrew,' said Mum, nicking a chip from Andrew's plate. Andrew rolled his eyes.

'The things I put up with in this house,' he said.

'Poor old boy,' said Mum, 'good job we love you then, isn't it?'

It took all day Saturday to build the hawk's cage.

'It's called a mews,' Colin told Andrew.

'Ooooh, posh! How d'you know that?'

'Mum got me a book out of the library.'

'Reading? You?' said Andrew. 'Phew. You'll be writing next. Come on, Shakespeare, we got some more wire to nail if this girlfriend of yours is going to have room to fly.'

Mr Scorsby brought the hawk up in the dark and put her on her perch in the big new cage.

'I brought her feeding bowl,' he said, 'they like a bit of routine. Move it a bit further from her each day, see if that'll persuade her to fly.'

The vet had brought a supply of dead rabbits too.

'Let me know how you get on,' he said, 'and I'll still need help in the surgery sometimes, remember!'

They'd covered the back of the cage with sacking so the hawk couldn't see the comings and going from the house. Colin spent most of the day peeping at her through the holes, watching to see if she'd fly. She didn't. She jumped down to her feedbowl for her supper and didn't get back up to her perch. She slept on the ground. Colin worried that if a fox got through the wire in the night, she'd be eaten.

It was light at six the next morning and Colin went straight out to the hawk. She was walking around in the grass on the bottom of her cage. She looked like an old lady paddling with her skirts tucked into her knickers. It was funny, but not dignified. Colin wanted to see her flying like a real bird. He decided not to give her breakfast and came up with a new plan for the evening.

Mum helped him slide the bird table into the cage. The hawk screamed and huddled at the back of the cage, but when she'd stopped, Colin put the blue feeding bowl, with a nice joint of rabbit in it, on the bird table.

If she wanted to eat, she'd have to fly.

The hawk stared at the bowl. She walked around the base of the bird table and scratched at it with her long legs. She chittered a bit, then walked to the end of the cage and started preening with her back to the food. Then she turned round and looked at it again. This time she tensed her wings so the joints jutted forward and quite suddenly stretched them out and started to flap! It was more of a scramble than a flight up to the bird table, but it was a start.

Every afternoon for a fortnight, Colin put the hawk's blue food bowl up on the bird table and the hawk flew from her perch to the table and back again. With every flight he could see she was growing stronger.

Then, one day after school when Colin came to feed her, he saw that a chaffinch had got into the cage and was fluttering about, trying to find a way out. Colin watched through the spy hole to see what the hawk would do. Her eyes blazed like the inside of a volcano and she shot down the cage in a swift glide; when the chaffinch turned to escape her, she turned faster. The white patch on her old injury flashed as she grabbed it with her claws.

'Trust me, Colin,' said Mr Scorsby, 'if she can fly and she can catch birds, then she's ready.'

Colin swept the dust on the surgery floor into a pile.

'But what if she isn't strong enough to hunt every day?'

'That's why you'll leave a bit of food out for her at first,' said Mr Scorsby, 'until she's really found her form again. Falconers call it hacking back.'

Colin looked up. He liked the special words to do with hawks and falconry; Mr Scorsby smiled.

'It really works, Colin. She'll be fine. You've done a great job.'

Colin cycled home, thinking about the hawk all the way: her flame-coloured eyes; the butter-cream and bark-brown of her feathers; the way she'd turned, so fast, to snatch that chaffinch out of the air. She had changed him. He noticed things now he'd never noticed before: the buzzards that soared over the hills; the kestrals hovering above the field edges and, once, a sparrowhawk gliding down the lane in front of his bike, so close to the ground it could have been skating on the tarmac.

No one at school called him names any more. Instead, they asked all sorts of questions about the hawk. How old was she? How long would she live? What did she hunt in the wild? At first Colin hadn't known the answers, but he had found out. Reading was useful when there was stuff you really wanted to know. At the end of one afternoon, Mrs Calvin had said that they weren't going to have a story, but that Colin was going to tell them all about 'Native Birds of Prey'. He had stood up in front of the whole class and talked.

Things at home were different, too. Mum didn't treat him like a baby any more. Now, even when Andrew was home, it was Colin who brought the logs in from the shed, or carried the shopping.

'Well, pardner,' Andrew said in his awful American accent, 'good to have another man about the house!'

At mealtimes, Mum and Andrew didn't bicker over Colin's head as they used to. Instead, the three of them talked together. Andrew had always made them laugh, but now Mum made them all laugh with her stories of the mad things that people at her work did. They talked about the hawk too. Mum and Andrew really liked to hear how she was doing, and even came out to the cage to look at her sometimes. For the first time in a very, very long time, the three of them felt like a real family.

When Colin got home he left his bike by the back door and went to look at the hawk through the peephole in the sack-covered end of her cage. She was sitting on the bird table, looking out at the fields and trees. She held her wings a little away from her body and her legs were bent, poised, ready for her to jump into flight. His foot broke a twig and she turned towards the sound. She couldn't see him, of course, but he could see her, right into the fierce, wild heart of those burning eyes. Mr Scorsby was right, she was ready.

Quietly, Colin slipped around to the other end of her cage, unhooked the latch on the door and then pushed it open with a stick so that she wouldn't see him. There was now nothing between her and freedom.

At first she didn't seem to notice, and then some blue tits scolding each other in a bush caught her attention. She watched them intently for a few moments and then, very suddenly, took off from the bird table. She was gone, in one long glide that took her low over the grass, then lifted her effortlessly clear of the fence. He followed her dark shape, growing smaller and smaller, along the hedgerow, and then lost it against the tangle of branches and the dots of the first new leaves as she reached the copse.

For a long time, Colin stood looking after her, staining his eyes in the clear light. He didn't know whether to laugh, or shout, or cry.

Colin saw her come back once for the bit of rabbit he left in her opened cage. A second joint of rabbit disappeared a few days later, but he couldn't be sure it had been the hawk who took it. He went on putting out meat every two days for a month, but mostly they were left untouched. The day Colin caught a fox shaking the bird table to knock the meat to the floor, he stopped putting food out.

'I'm sure she's fine!' Mum said.

'Yeah,' said Andrew, 'bet she's stuffing herself on little birds, no need for manky bits of rabbit out of our freezer.'

But Colin wasn't so hopeful. He feared her injury had made her weak, and that in spite of all his care and his struggle to right the wrong he had done, she had still died.

Spring turned to summer. Andrew sold the air rifle and used the money to buy Colin binoculars. Through them,

Colin saw buzzard chicks exercising their wings in their nest at the top of the tallest oak tree in the copse, and tiny roe deer fawns tottering beside their mums in the hay meadow.

Everyday after school, he helped out at Mr Scorsby's evening surgery. Mostly people brought dogs and cats, but Colin liked it best when there were wild animals to tend to: a litter of newborn hedgehogs that needed feeding with an eye dropper; a jackdaw with a broken wing; a stunned thrush that he fed on worms for two days and then released in the Scorsby's garden.

'Better work at your sciences when you go to big school in the autumn, ' Mr Scorsby told him. 'You're a vet in the making, that's for sure!'

Colin felt his life was opening out, like a map unfolding, revealing all sorts of places and directions that he had never thought of before.

And yet, a part of his heart was heavy with guilt and regret, thinking about his hawk.

Then, on the last day of term, he got a puncture on the way to school. He left the bike behind a hedge to pick up on the way home and walked down the hill into the village. The morning sunlight slanted and pricked between the leaves of the beech trees that leaned over the lane from the top of the hedge bank. Small birds, tits and chaffinches were making a fuss in a hawthorn bush in front of him, a sign,

Colin had learned, that a bird of prey was nearby. Then a male blackbird broke cover and flew into the empty lane right in front of him. Instantly, it was snatched from the air. One moment the blackbird was there, and the next there was simply a puff of feathers floating to the ground, so fast it was like a conjuring trick. In the old days, Colin would hardly have noticed it. But his senses were tuned in now, aware of all the life around him, so in the split second it took the hawk to shoot out of the hedge and grab its prey, Colin had seen the fierce, wild eyes and the unmistakeable flash of white on the left wing.

He picked up a sooty blackbird feather from where it had fallen to the ground and put it in his pocket then walked on down the hill, his heart soaring and gliding, up through the canopy of green into a clear blue sky.

Nicola Davies

Nicola is an award-winning author whose many books for children include *The Promise* (Green Earth Book Award 2015, CILIP Kate Greenaway Medal Shortlist 2015), *Tiny* (AAAS/Subaru SB&F Prize 2015), *A First Book of Nature, Whale Boy* (Blue Peter Book Awards Shortlist 2014), and the Heroes of the Wild series (Portsmouth Book Award 2014). She graduated in Zoology, studied whales and bats and then worked for the BBC Natural History Unit. Underlying all Nicola's writing is the belief that a relationship with nature is essential to every human being, and that now, more than ever, we need to renew that relationship.

Nicola's children's books from Graffeg include *Perfect* (2017 CILIP Kate Greenaway Medal Longlist), *The Pond* (2018 CILIP Kate Greenaway Medal Longlist), the Shadows and Light series, *The Word Bird, Animal Surprises* and *Into the Blue.*

Cathy Fisher

Cathy Fisher grew up with eight brothers and sisters, playing in the fields overlooking Bath. She has been a teacher and practising artist all her life, living and working in the UK, Seychelles and Australia.

Art is Cathy's first language. As a young child she scribbled on the walls of her bedroom and ever since has felt a sense of urgency to paint and draw stories which she feels need to be heard and expressed.

Cathy's first published books with Graffeg include *Perfect*, followed by *The Pond*, written by Nicola Davies. Both books were Longlisted for the CILIP Kate Greenaway Medal.

Flying Free
Published in Great Britain in 2018
by Graffeg Limited

Written by Nicola Davies
copyright © 2018.
Illustrated by Cathy Fisher
copyright © 2018.
Designed and produced by Graffeg
Limited copyright © 2018.

Graffeg Limited, 24 Stradey Park
Business Centre, Mwrwg Road,
Llangennech, Llanelli, Carmarthenshire
SA14 8YP Wales UK
Tel 01554 824000 www.graffeg.com

ISBN 9781912654093

1 2 3 4 5 6 7 8 9